SNAIL
HAS LUNCH

by MARY PETERSON

ALADDIN PIX

NEW YORK   LONDON   TORONTO   SYDNEY   NEW DELHI

ALADDIN PIX

Simon & Schuster Children's Publishing Division
1230 Avenue of the Americas, New York, New York 10020
First Aladdin PIX hardcover edition September 2016
For information about special discounts for bulk purchases, please contact
Simon & Schuster Special Sales at 1-866-506-1949 or business@simonandschuster.com.
The Simon & Schuster Speakers Bureau can bring authors to your live event.
For more information or to book an event contact the Simon & Schuster Speakers Bureau
at 1-866-248-3049 or visit our website at www.simonspeakers.com.
Book designed by Karina Granda
The illustrations for this book were rendered digitally.
The text of this book was set in Archer.
Manufactured in China 0616 SCP
2 4 6 8 10 9 7 5 3 1
Library of Congress Control Number 2015960931
ISBN 978-1-4814-5302-8 (hc)
ISBN 978-1-4814-5303-5 (eBook)

For my sweet (and spicy!) daughter,
Jenna

CHAPTER 1

Snail lived in a bucket.

He loved his old rusty bucket.

WARM IN
WINTER

COOL IN
SUMMER

DRY WHEN
IT RAINS

AND CHOCK-FULL OF
BROWN GRASS AND DIRT

He was so comfy he had no reason
to leave his bucket.

Ever.

Mmmm.
Bland.

Nearly every afternoon, Snail's friend Ladybug would come by. Sometimes she would tell him stories about her friends . . .

Then Rabbit raced Squirrel to the pear tree, hopping backward.

or stories about the newest
tasty treat in the garden. . . .

Every visit, Ladybug would try to convince
Snail to leave his bucket.

Would you like to come in and have some brown grass and dirt with me?

IN?
Brown grass and dirt?

Snail, the sun is shining!

The pea pods are crunchy!

The birds are chirping!

The strawberries
are super-sweet!

THINKING.

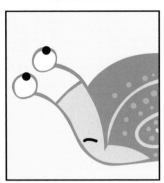

PONDERING.

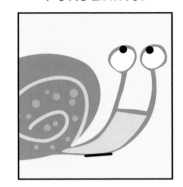

CONSIDERING.

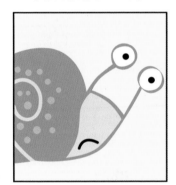

RUMINATING.

Ladybug was disappointed
and went on her way.

Snail would soon find out.

CHAPTER 2

Snail had no idea what had happened.

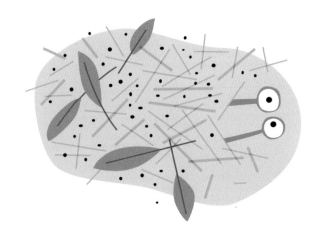

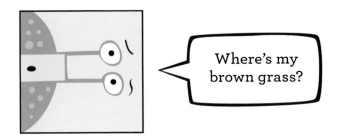

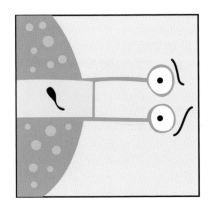

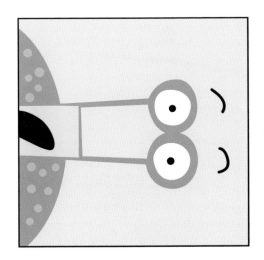

Just then a shadow passed
over Snail's face.

He shut his eyes tight,
hoping it would disappear.

Arrgh!

Don't
hurt me!

Stay
away!

Relax, Snail!
It's just me.

Snail opened
his eyes and saw
his best friend.

But Snail wouldn't budge. There was
only one place he wanted to go: **HOME!**

Snail was scared.
But he was also hungry.

Wait
for me!

Slowly but not so surely,
he followed Ladybug from . . .

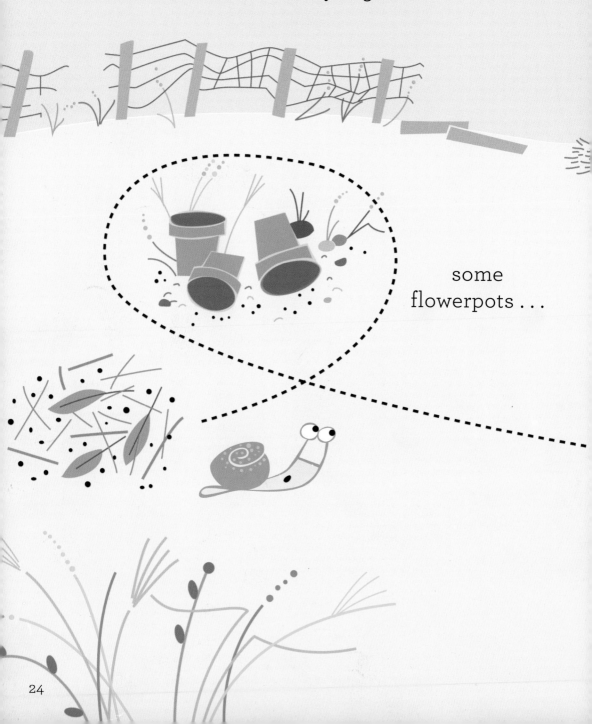

some
flowerpots . . .

to a tree
stump . . .

past a pair of
dirty boots . . .

to the . . .

25

CHAPTER 3

Garden!

Snail couldn't believe his eyes.
Everything was so colorful.

Snail didn't know where to begin.

First he nibbled on a pea pod.

Next a beet.

The yellow tomato was a tasty surprise.

But the rhubarb was . . .

At that moment a bunch of little red something-or-others caught Snail's eye.

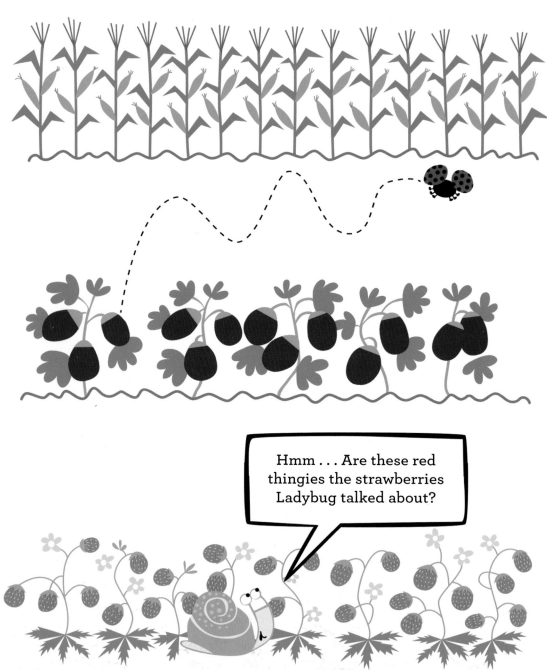

Hmm . . . Are these red thingies the strawberries Ladybug talked about?

They smelled nice.
They looked tasty.
Snail took a bite and . . .
he was in heaven.

So sweet.

Ladybug!
Guess what? I think
I just tasted your
strawberries.

You were right.
They are delicious!

Ladybug?

Since this was Snail's first time in the garden,
he didn't know Ladybug was only one row over.

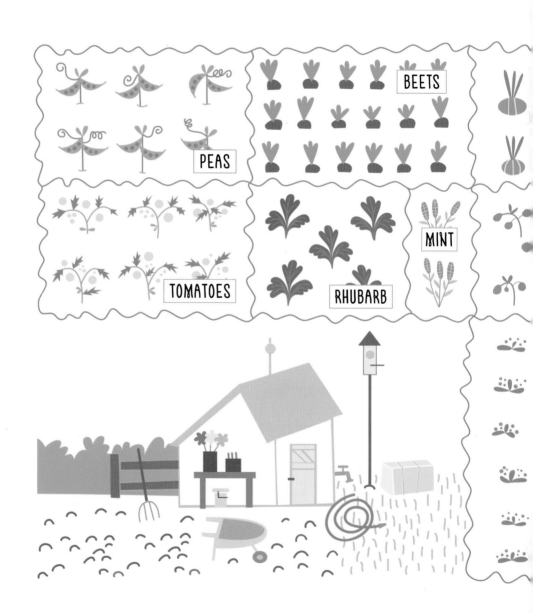

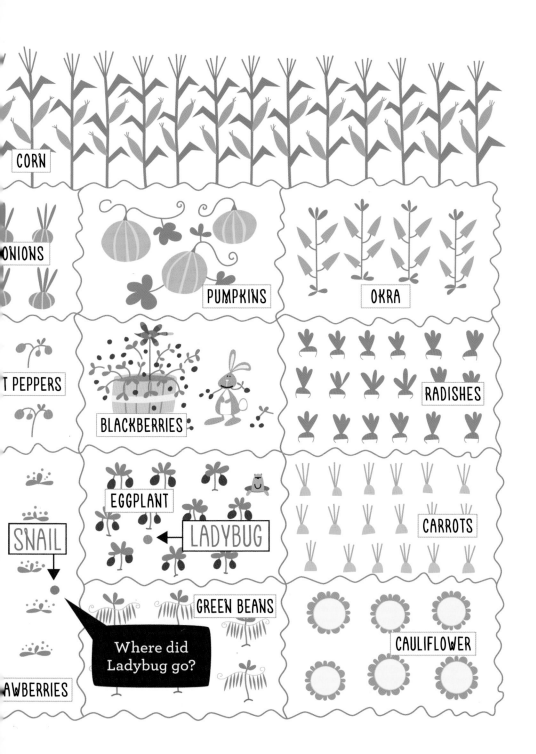

CORN

ONIONS

PUMPKINS

OKRA

T PEPPERS

BLACKBERRIES

RADISHES

EGGPLANT

LADYBUG

CARROTS

SNAIL

GREEN BEANS

Where did Ladybug go?

CAULIFLOWER

AWBERRIES

33

Snail looked
under the
green beans,

Where
is she?

inside the cauliflower,

and around the carrots.

Will I ever see Ladybug again?

And then he looked up right into . . .

CHAPTER 4

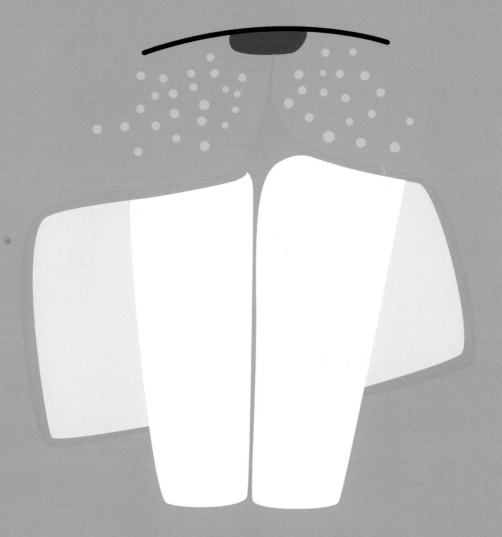

Two big teeth.

For the second time that day,
Snail closed his eyes.

Snail couldn't believe how Gopher stuffed his cheeks.

When Gopher was finally finished, Snail asked . . .

Have you seen Ladybug?

Never met her.

This wasn't good news.

Well then, Mr. Gopher, maybe you've seen my bucket?

Bucket? Bucket?

Hey, Rabbit! Have you seen this kid's bucket?

Snail looked past Gopher and saw another furry creature. This one was bigger and had long ears.

What a ridiculous question. There must be fifteen buckets in this garden.

BIG ROUND ORANGE BUCKET

SMALL RED BUCKET WITH A HOLE

STORAGE BUCKET WITH A SNAP LID

USED PAINT BUCKET

WOODEN WATER BUCKET

OLD RUSTY BUCKET

Snail's eyes got wide.

Did you say "old rusty bucket"?

Rabbit took a bite from a blackberry.

Snail was about to cry.

It's just past the pumpkins. I'll take you there after this last bite.

Snail grinned from eyeball to eyeball.

Soon he would be home. And he hoped Ladybug would be there waiting for him.

CHAPTER 5

When Rabbit finished his blackberries,
he quickly led the way. Snail moved as fast
as he could, but he was a snail, after all.

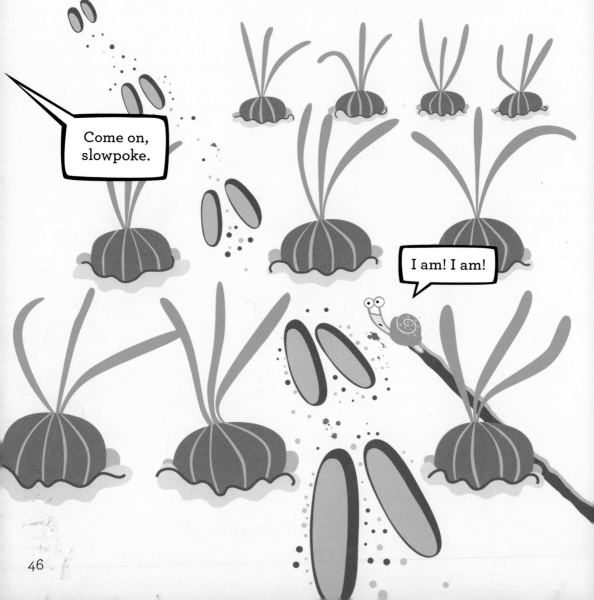

Right past the onions, another pretty
little red strawberry appeared in front of him.

Just one more taste,
and I'll hurry home.

Now, if Snail had ever left his cozy little bucket,
he would have known that was not a
sweet and delicious strawberry.

What he was about to eat . . .

was a pretty little RED HOT PEPPER.

Luckily for Snail, Ladybug heard his cry.

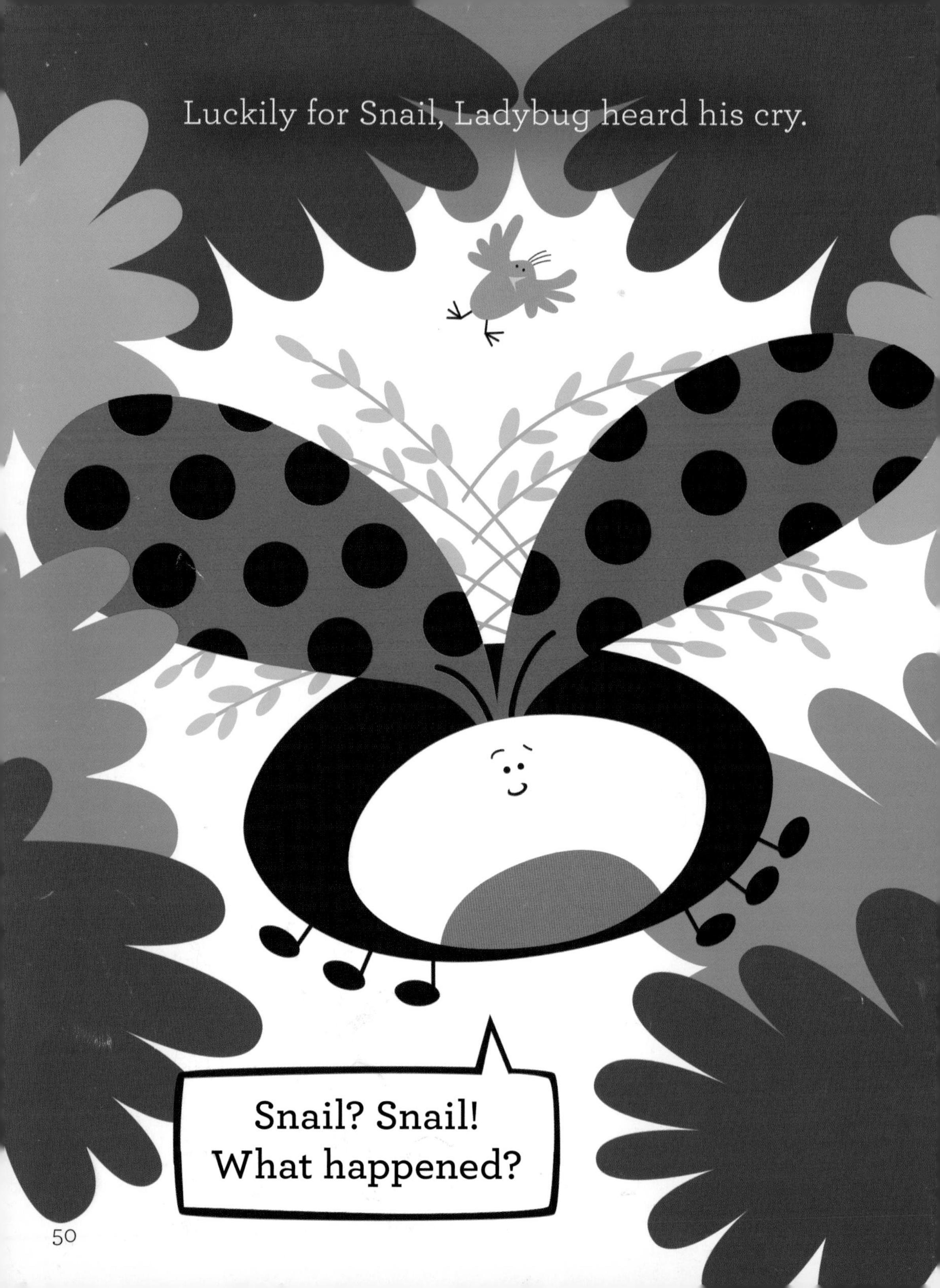

51

Be careful with the pretty little peppers. They may be cute, but they are spicy!

Snail was not happy.

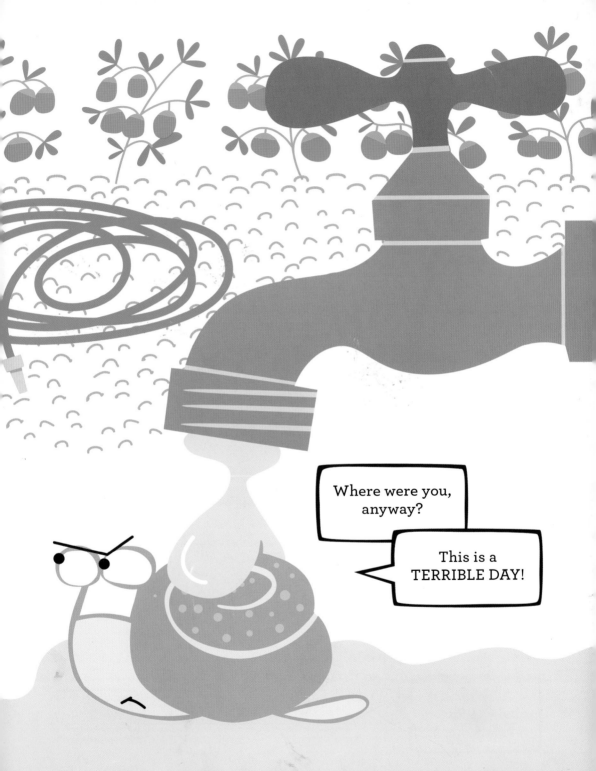

Ladybug was shocked.

Maybe Ladybug had a point. Snail looked dreamily toward the strawberry patch and couldn't believe his eyes.

Ladybug, LOOK! There's my bucket!

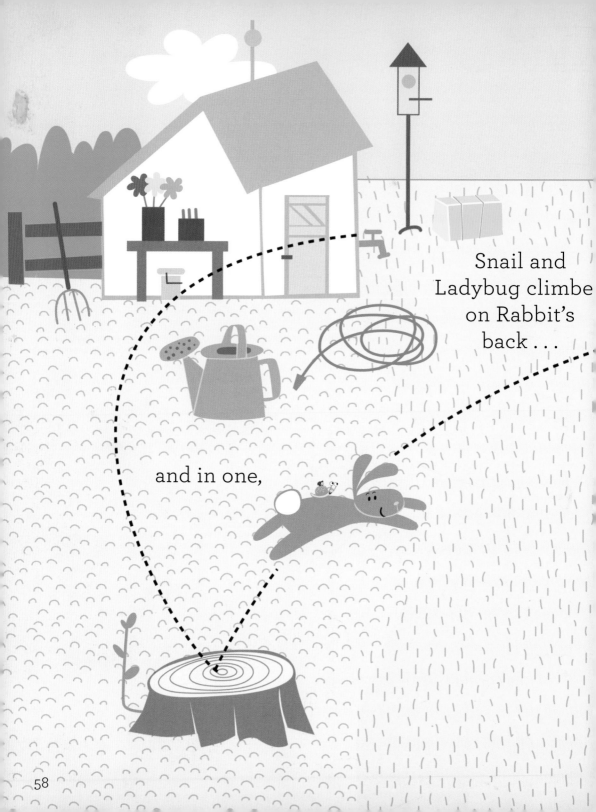

Snail and
Ladybug climbe
on Rabbit's
back . . .

and in one,

two,

three hops,

they were at the bucket.

Snail was confused. The bucket was old and rusty, but it was filled with **STRAWBERRIES!**

Wait a minute. Whose bucket is this?

It's yours, silly.

Oh, Snail!

Mary Peterson is an illustrator of many books for young readers, including *Dig In!*, *Piggies in the Pumpkin Patch*, *Wiggle and Waggle*, and *Wooby & Peep*. She lives in Los Angeles, California.